A Bea

BETSY BYARS was born in cotton-mill worker. Although she read a great deal as a child, she didn't want to be a writer, but to work with animals. She began writing when her own children were small and has now written more than thirty books for children, including the *Blossom* series which is published in Macmillan Children's Books. A hugely successful author on both sides of the Atlantic, she has won the Newbery Medal and the American Book Award. She lives in Clemson, South Carolina, and is a licensed pilot.

Betsy Byars

A Bean Birthday

Illustrated by
Kate Aldous

MACMILLAN CHILDREN'S BOOKS

First published 1996 by Macmillan Children's Books
a division of Macmillan Publishers Limited
Cavaye Place London SW10 9PG
and Basingstoke
Associated companies worldwide

ISBN 0 330 33694 0

Text copyright © Betsy Byars 1996
Illustrations copyright © Kate Aldous 1996

The right of Betsy Byars to be identified as the
author of this work has been asserted by her in accordance
with the Copyright, Designs and Patents Act 1988.

9 8 7 6 5 4 3

A CIP catalogue record for this book is available
from the British Library

Typeset in 12½/18 Berthold Baskerville BE
DTP by Nigel Hazle
Printed by Mackays of Chatham PLC, Kent.

Contents

A Mad Bean

"Mama."

Anna ran up the steps. She ran into the living-room.

"Mama!"

She slammed the door behind her.

Mrs Bean came into the room. "Anna, please don't slam the door."

"I couldn't help it, Mama. I am mad!"

"Why? What happened?"

"I am too mad to tell! Yaaaaangh!

"Calm down, Anna. Let's talk about it."

"Wait for me!" Jenny Bean called from the kitchen. "I want to hear this."

George Bean called, "Wait for me, too."

Jenny and George ran into the living-room. Both of them had seen Anna mad before. She

always got mad when they messed with her things. But nobody had seen Anna mad enough to slam doors and yell, "Yaaaaangh."

"Go ahead. Tell it," Jenny said. Her eyes

shone with excitement. "What happened?

"I want to know, too," George said.

Mrs Bean said, "Yes, don't keep us waiting, Anna. What happened?"

"Well," Anna began, "there is this new boy in my room at school."

She stopped. She made her hands into fists. "I am so mad I can't even tell it!"

"Calm down, Anna. Start over," Mrs Bean suggested.

"I am so mad I don't know where I was."

"There is this new boy in your room at school," Jenny said.

"Yes, there is this new boy in my school."

"And has this boy done something?" Mrs Bean asked.

"Yes!"

"What?" Jenny asked quickly.

"This new boy at school has started calling me—" Anna broke off. "You know how much I hate nicknames. It makes me so mad."

"What does he call you, Anna?" Jenny asked eagerly.

"He calls me—" Anna broke off again. "I don't want to say it. It's too awful."

"What?" the Beans asked together.

"He calls me Anna Banana!"

Mrs Bean smiled. "Is that all?"

"Is that all? Is that all? How would you like to be Anna Banana?"

George said, "The kids at school call me String Bean, and I don't mind."

Jenny said, "They call me Jelly Bean and I like it."

"Well, I hate Anna Banana. I hate it! It makes me feel like a lady ape."

"Anna, listen," said Mrs Bean. "If you let this boy see that it bothers you—"

"It does bother me! I hate it! Anna Banana! Yuck!"

Mrs Bean began again. "Anna, if you let this boy see that it bothers you, he will keep on calling you Anna Banana."

"He is going to keep on no matter what I do. And he doesn't just go, 'Anna Banana', like that. He goes, 'Anna Ba-naaaaaaa-na!' I hate it, and I'm afraid everyone is going to start calling me that."

"Listen, Anna. If you pretend that it doesn't bother you, the boy will stop. It's as simple as that."

"How can I pretend it doesn't bother me? It does bother me a lot."

"I'll show you how to pretend," Jenny offered.

"What?"

"I'll show you how to pretend that it doesn't bother you. I'm going to be an actress, you know. Here's the way an actress would do it."

"Yes, watch Jenny," Mrs Bean said.

Jenny said, "An actress would do it like this." She started walking across the living-room.

"Now, George," she said over her shoulder, "you pretend to be the boy. Go, 'Anna Ba-naaaaa-na!'"

George said, "Anna Ba-naaaaa-na!"

"He does it louder than that," Anna said.

George said it louder. "Anna Ba-naaaaaaaa-na!"

Jenny turned. She didn't look at George. She looked over the top of his head. Then, as if she had not seen anybody, she turned around. She walked away.

"See, Anna," Jenny said, "you look at him as if he is not there. George, didn't you feel like you weren't there? Like you were nothing?"

George said, "Yes."

"Go on, Anna, try it on George."

"I don't like to feel like I'm nothing," George admitted.

"See, Anna. It worked. Go ahead, George."

George sighed. He said, "Anna Banaaaaaaaa-na!"

"Oh, it's no use," Anna said. "Maybe I could look at George as if he isn't there, but it doesn't make me mad when a Bean goes, 'Anna Banaaaaa-na'. It just makes me mad when this boy does."

"You have to rehearse," Jenny said. "Even stars have to rehearse. Try it, Anna."

Anna shook her head. "No."

Anna paused. Then she looked up.

"But I can tell you one thing," she said.

"What?" Jenny asked.

"If this boy calls me Anna Banana one more time, he's going to be sorry."

Jenny came closer. Her eyes shone. "Why? What are you going to do to him?"

George came closer, too.

"Now, Anna," warned Mrs Bean.

Anna's eyes darkened. Her lips tightened.

"What are you going to do?" Jenny asked. "You have to tell us. What are you going to do?"

Anna sighed.

She looked out the window.

In a small voice she said, "I don't know."

Beans in the Wardrobe

Mrs Bean went back into the kitchen. Jenny waited until her mother was gone.

Then in a low voice she said, "Anna, I can make you forget about being called Anna Banana."

Anna said, "Nobody can make me forget that."

"I bet I can."

"How?"

"I know a secret.

"What?"

"You won't tell?"

"I have never told a secret in my life," said Anna. She looked interested.

"I won't tell either," George said quickly.

Jenny glanced at the kitchen door to make

sure Mrs Bean couldn't hear.

"Let's go in the hall," she said. "I don't want Mama to hear. The secret's about her. Also, that's where the secret is."

"In the hall?" George asked.

Jenny nodded, and George and Anna followed her into the hall.

Jenny stopped at the wardrobe door. She turned. Her eyes were shining.

"What is the secret?" George asked.

Jenny opened the wardrobe door. She pulled aside the clothes. She pointed to a box at the back of the wardrobe.

"That is the secret," she said.

The box was round. There was a big red bow on top.

"The secret is a box?" George asked.

"The secret is what's in the box."

"What is in it?" George asked.

"A present."

George looked more interested. George loved presents. "Who is it for?" he asked hopefully.

"It's for Mama. It's her birthday plesent."

George said, "Oh."

"I found it yesterday," Jenny said. "I was looking for my skates. I asked Papa about it. Papa said it was Mama's birthday present."

"What is it?" Anna asked. "Did he say?"

Jenny leaned around the door and glanced at the kitchen to make sure Mrs Bean couldn't hear. She lowered her voice.

"Promise you won't tell."

"I promise," Anna said.

"Me too," George said quickly.

"Dishes."

"Dishes!"

"Be quiet, Anna. Do you want Mama to hear?"

"I can't believe it's dishes. Mama has enough dishes."

"Well, now she's going to have more," Jenny said.

"I don't believe it."

"It's true. They are big round dishes with flowers on them."

"Papa never gives Mama things like dishes," Anna said. "He always gives her something for herself."

"Well, this year it's dishes."

"He told you that?"

"Not exactly," Jenny admitted. "He let me guess. And when I guessed dishes, he winked at me." Jenny grinned. "Now I know what everybody is giving Mama."

She began to count on her fingers.

"Papa's giving dishes. I am making Mama a pot holder. I'm knitting it. It's that long."

Jenny measured three inches in the air. Then she went on. "You're giving her a poem," she said to Anna.

"How do you know that?" Anna asked.

"I saw you writing it. It's called 'Mama's Birthday.'"

"You don't know what I'm giving," George said.

"You always give Mama flowers. You pick them out of people's gardens," Jenny said.

George looked unhappy.

"Only you'd better not pick them out of people's gardens this year," she went on. "They might call the police."

"I won't."

"In past years you could get away with it. You were little then. This year you're too big."

"I won't! If I can't find flowers this year, I will draw a picture of flowers."

"Children," Mrs Bean called, "I need some help."

Jenny closed the wardrobe door.

"Now, remember," she said, "You both promised not to tell."

"I have never told a secret in my life," Anna said again.

"I've told them before," George admitted. "But I won't tell this one."

"All right," Jenny said, "let's go see what Mama wants. Act like we never heard of presents."

"We're coming, Mama," she called.

As they went into the living-room, Anna said, "You were right, Jenny."

"About what?"

"The secret did make me forget about Anna Banana."

"I knew it would." Jenny paused. "Anyway, Anna," she said, "I know where he got it from. He didn't just make it up."

"Where did he get it?"

"It's from a skipping song I know. Want to hear it?"

"I guess so."

"Anna Banana
Plays the piano
All she knows is 'The Star Spangled Banner'."

Anna said, "Yaaaaangh! I'm getting mad all over again. I hate being Anna Banana."

"I can understand that," Jenny admitted. "It's not nearly as nice as being Jelly Bean."

Beans in the Kitchen

"George," Mrs Bean called, "come into the kitchen, please."

George came into the kitchen slowly. He did not want to come at all. George had known the secret about his mother's present for two days, and for two days he had been worried about telling her.

Mrs Bean was at the sink. She was peeling potatoes.

"Have you finished your homework, George?" Mrs Bean asked.

"Almost."

George sat down at the table. He hooked his feet behind the chair legs.

He watched his mother. Then he said, "Saturday is your birthday."

He did not know why he had said that. He did *not* want to talk about birthdays.

"I know," she said.

"Are you excited, Mama?"

"Yes, I am. I love birthdays, because when I

was growing up, we didn't have them."

"You didn't have birthdays?" George asked.

"We had birthdays, but we didn't have parties. We didn't get presents."

"You didn't get any presents?" George asked.

"Well, my mother would buy me a pair of shoes to wear to school and she would say, 'Now, these are for your birthday', even though my birthday was months away."

"You got shoes for your birthday? Shoes?"

"There were eleven of us George, remember? Getting a new pair of shoes was a treat."

"So I guess you really like your birthdays now."

"Yes, George, I do."

"Everybody in this family is giving you a present – and no shoes, either."

"Well, don't tell, George. That would ruin the surprise."

"Oh, I am not going to tell you. I promise. I wouldn't tell if you begged me."

"I won't beg."

"And I won't tell."

Mrs Bean put the potatoes in a pot. In the silence that followed, George said, "I won't tell no matter what."

"That makes me proud of you. I know how hard it is for you to keep a secret."

"It's very hard," George admitted. "But you can beg and beg, and I still won't tell you. All I will say is that Anna is giving you *one* thing – she made it up herself. Jenny is giving you *one* thing – she made it herself. I am giving you *some* things. Papa is giving you *some* things too, but he bought his. That is my last word on presents."

"Good. I really don't like to know. The surprise makes it fun."

Anna came into the flat. She slammed the front door and ran into the kitchen.

"Anna—"

"I couldn't help slamming the door!" Anna said. She pulled off her sweater and threw it on the table.

"Guess what? He's done it again!" she said.

"Who? What?"

"That stupid boy."

"Don't call people stupid, Anna. You know I don't like that."

"I'm sorry, Mama, but it's the truth. This boy is stupid. Listen to what he did."

"Now, Anna—"

Jenny ran into the kitchen. "Wait for me. I want to hear, too. Go ahead. I'm ready," she said.

"I was walking down the street. I stopped to look in a shop window. Someone behind me said, 'Anna Ba-naaaaa-na.' I knew it was that stupid—" She glanced at her mother. "I knew it was that boy. I could see his reflection in the glass."

Jenny asked, "What colour hair does he have?"

"Red."

"I knew it would be red! Go on."

"Did you pretend it didn't bother you?" Mrs Bean asked.

"I pretended I didn't hear him."

"Good for you."

"I just kept on looking at the things in the shop window."

"Show me," Jenny said. "Act it out. Pretend that the stove is the shop window."

Anna turned to the cooker.

"I was standing like this. He was standing right about there."

"I'll be the boy," Jenny said quickly.

"I pretended I hadn't heard him so he did it again."

Jenny said, "'Anna Ba-naaaaaa-na!' Does that sound like him?"

"Sort of. I kept standing there, looking in the window. Then he said, 'What's the matter, Anna Banana? Don't you know your name?'"

"Let me," Jenny said. "'What's the matter, Anna Banana? Don't you know your name?'"

"That sounds just like him," Anna said.

Jenny said, "Thank you."

"So I stopped looking in the window. I turned around, like this. I looked right over his head, like this. Then I walked away, like this."

Anna walked towards the living-room with her

head high. She stopped at the door. She turned.

"How did I do?" she asked.

"Wonderful!" said Mrs Bean.

"I couldn't have done it better myself," Jenny said. "And I'm the Bean actress."

"I liked it, too," said George.

"Thank you, thank you," Anna said.

She bowed to the Beans, and the Beans clapped.

One Bean in the Basement

George Bean was worried.

George Bean was very worried.

Just being around dishes worried George these days. Now he was drying them. That was even worse.

George had not wanted to dry the dishes tonight. He knew that if he was drying dishes, he would be thinking about dishes. He might even start talking about new dishes.

He had begged, "Please, please, I'll do anything that doesn't have to do with dishes."

But Mr Bean had said, "George, dry the dishes for your mother," in a stern way. So now George was drying the dishes. He dried two cups and put them in the rack.

To take his mind off dishes, George said to his

mother, "I am not going to tell you what you're getting for your birthday."

Mrs Bean said, "Good. Let's talk about something else. Tell me about school today."

George dried a dish and a glass.

He said, "I am not even going to give you a hint."

"I'm so glad. Now what happened at school today? Did you have maths?"

"All I will say is that the things you are getting are round and you eat off them."

George gasped.

Mrs Bean dropped a pan. George dropped the towel.

Then there was a terrible silence.

George covered his mouth with his hands, but it was too late. The words were already out.

Tears came to George's eyes. He bent down and picked up the towel. He wiped his face with the damp cloth.

He glanced at the door to see if anyone else had heard.

Mrs Bean began to sing. George knew she

was pretending she had not heard, but George knew that she had.

He dried the last two dishes. Then he said, "May I go?" His voice trembled.

"Yes, George." Mrs Bean said in a kind voice.

George walked into the living-room. His father was singing along with the radio.

George passed his father. He reached for the door knob, but he missed. The tears in his eyes blinded him.

George did not want to wipe away his tears. His father might see him. He did not want his father to ask, "Why are you crying, George?"

Mr Bean stopped singing as George reached for the door knob a second time.

"Where are you going, son?"

George said, "Out."

"Be back before dark."

"I will."

"Have you done your homework?"

"Yes."

Jenny jumped up from the sofa. "Can I come with you, George?"

"No."

"Why not? I've finished my homework and my reading. Please, George."

"No."

"Why not? I don't have anything to do. I—"

"I need to be by myself," George said.

He opened the door, went out and shut the

door behind him. Then he ran down the steps, both flights.

He stopped at the bottom of the steps and listened. He was afraid Jenny might be following him. She would want to know what was wrong. She would make him tell. She would keep after him until he did.

No, the hall was quiet. His shoulders sagged. Jenny had not followed him. Nobody had. The hall was empty.

George crossed the hall.

There was a door behind the steps that led to the basement. George opened that door.

He paused. He looked down the basement steps and took a breath of cold basement air.

The basement was dark. Only a little light came in through the high, thin windows.

George shivered. Then he went down three steps and closed the door. Slowly, he went down the rest of the steps.

The basement was dirty and spidery. It was full of old forgotten boxes and things nobody wanted any more.

George sat on the bottom step.

It was just the place, George thought, for a boy who had ruined his mother's birthday.

Beans on the Stairs

"I'm going to look for George," Jenny said.

"Why are you going to look for George?" Mr Bean asked. "Is George missing?"

"Yes, and I think something's wrong with him."

"Why do you think that?" Mr Bean asked. He turned down the radio.

"When something is wrong with a Bean, I always know. And he might even have been crying."

"George? Crying?"

"I think so. Didn't you hear his voice tremble?"

Mr Bean got up at once. He crossed the room and opened the door.

"George!" he called down the stairs.

There was no answer.

Mr Bean went out and stood at the top of the stairs.

"George! Yoo-hoo! Where are you, son?"

Again there was no answer.

Mr Bean went back into the living-room. He said, "Jenny, do you have any idea where your brother went?"

"No, he just said he needed to be by himself. Those were his very words."

"It's not like George to want to be alone," Mr Bean said.

"You want me to go look for him, Papa? I will. I'll go right now."

"Maybe you'd better, Jenny."

Anna came into the living-room then. "Did you say you are going out to look for George?"

"Yes."

"Wait. I'll go with you." Anna glanced around. "Where is my blue sweater?"

"Right there."

"And do you have a comb I could use? My hair is—"

"Anna, you are not going to a dance," Mr Bean snapped. "You are going to look for your brother."

"I know, Papa. I still want to look nice."

"You don't have to look nice to find your brother."

"Somebody might see me," Anna said. She paused to look in the mirror.

"We could see that red-headed boy," she said to Jenny. "If we do, I'll show him to you."

"I hope we do see him," said Jenny. "I want to hear him call you Anna Banana."

"Girls!" Mr Bean threw up his hands.

Anna and Jenny turned to look at him.

"I am not sending you out to look for red-headed boys. I am sending you to look for your brother."

"We know that, Papa," Jenny said.

Anna went out the door saying, "I think he lives on Oak Street – the red-headed boy. We could look for George up that way."

"George is probably right out in front of the flat, and we won't get to go anywhere."

"The three of us could take a walk."

"Well," Jenny said, "I would like to see the red-headed boy."

"I wouldn't!" Anna pushed up the sleeves of her sweater.

"I want to hear him call you Anna Banana," Jenny said.

"Well, I don't." Anna pulled her sleeves down.

She and Jenny stepped outside. They stopped and looked up the street.

Kids were playing football. George was not with them. They looked down the street. Kids were playing tag. George was not with them either.

"I wonder where he could be," Anna said.

"I don't know. Let's walk over to Oak Street. Maybe we'll see him there."

"Who?" Anna asked.

Jenny grinned. "Both of them."

They walked fast, but they did not see George or the red-headed boy.

When they got back to their front steps, Anna said, "We'd better go tell Papa we couldn't find him."

"He probably came home while we were walking. I'll go and see."

Anna ran up the stairs. Jenny waited. Suddenly she looked up. She knew where George was.

She was crossing the hall, on her way to the basement, when Anna called down the steps,

"He's not here."

Jenny called back, "I know."

"How?" Anna started down the steps.

"Well, every time George does something wrong, something that makes him cry, he goes down in the basement."

"In the basement. Yuck!"

"I know. I feel the same way, but that's George!"

"How do you know?"

"I saw him going down there when he broke Mama's vase." Jenny pointed to the landing. "You wait there. I'll look in the basement. If George is there, I'll give you a thumbs-up, like this." Jenny stuck her thumb in the air. "Then you go upstairs."

"What will I tell Papa?"

"Tell Papa that George and I are coming in five minutes."

"He'll want to know where you are."

"Well, don't tell him."

"I'll try not to, but you know Papa."

"Yes, I know Papa, but don't tell! If you do,

he'll be down in the basement with us."

Anna leaned over the banister and watched as Jenny crossed the hall. Jenny opened the basement door. She peered into the darkness.

There was George. He was sitting on the bottom step. He was slumped forward. His chin was in his hands.

Jenny looked up at Anna. She stuck her thumb in the air. Anna nodded. Then she went up the steps.

"We found him, Papa," she said. "He and Jenny will be up in five minutes."

Two Beans in the Basement

Jenny Bean cleared her throat.

"George?"

George did not turn around. He stared into the darkness of the basement.

"George?"

"Who is it?" he asked in a low voice.

"It's me – Jelly Bean. Can I come down?"

"What do you want to come down for?"

"I just want to sit on the steps with you."

George sighed. "Why would anybody want to sit on the steps with me?"

"I just do."

"Well, if you are determined to sit on the steps with me, I can't stop you," he said.

"Thanks."

Jenny went down the steps and sat beside

George. "Hi, String." She hugged her knees to keep warm.

"Hi."

There was a silence. Then Jenny leaned forward. "What did you do?" she asked.

"What makes you think I did something?"

George still had not looked at her.

"I have all the Beans figured out," Jenny said. "Every time you feel bad, you come down in the basement."

George said, "Oh."

"Every time Anna feels bad she goes in the bedroom. Every time I feel bad I go out and skip with my friends."

"Well, maybe I do feel bad," George admitted.

"Why? What did you do?"

"Maybe I didn't do anything. Maybe I just feel bad!"

"What – did – you – do?

"Nothing!"

George moaned. He put his hands over his face. He slumped forward.

"I did something terrible," he said.

"What?"

"It's so terrible I can't tell you."

"You can tell me anything, String."

"Not this."

"Anything!"

"If I tell you, you'll hate me."

"I could never hate you, String. You're one of my favourite Beans."

"Oh, yes, you could."

"I promise I won't hate you."

"A person can promise something . . ." George began. He could not finish. He tried again. "A person can promise something, and—" He still could not finish.

"A person can promise something and then break the promise. Is that what you're trying to say?"

George nodded.

"I would never break a promise." She crossed her heart. "I will never hate you. What did you do?"

"I told Mama about the dishes."

"What?" Jenny jumped to her feet. "What?"

"I told Mama about the dishes."

"The birthday dishes?"

He nodded.

"You couldn't! You didn't!"

"Well, I didn't tell. I gave her a hint."

"What was the hint?"

"I said," George went on miserably, "that she was getting something round that you ate off."

"George! You promised! You broke a promise."

"Well, so did you. You promised you wouldn't hate me, and you do. I can tell."

"I don't exactly hate you, String, but when I promised, I didn't know what a terrible thing you had done. Are you sure she heard you?"

"Yes, she heard me." George spoke in a rush. "I didn't want to tell, Jelly. I didn't! That's why I didn't want to dry the dishes. Remember? I begged not to dry the dishes."

"I remember," Jenny said.

"I knew that if I dried the dishes, I would be thinking about dishes. I knew that if I was thinking about dishes, I would start talking about dishes. I knew that if I started talking about dishes, I would tell . . ."

George trailed off.

In a low voice he added, "You can believe me or you can not believe me. But, Jell, I honestly could not help it. It slipped out before I could stop it."

"I believe you, String."

She sat back on the steps beside George. She bent forward.

George broke the silence. "Are you going to tell Papa?"

"No, String."

"Thanks, Jell."

"Don't thank me. I'm not going to tell Papa. You're going to do that yourself."

"Me?"

"Yes, George. You."

Three Beans in the Basement

"Anna, where are they?"

Anna did not raise her eyes.

"Anna, I want you to look at me."

Anna sighed. She looked at Mr Bean.

"That's better. Now where are George and Jenny?"

"They'll be here in a minute."

"Anna," Mr Bean said sternly, "this is the last time I am asking this question."

"Thank you, Papa."

"This is the last time I am asking this question, because this time you will give me the answer."

"In the basement."

"The basement?"

"Yes, Papa."

"What are my children doing in the basement? Beans do not belong in a basement."

Mr Bean got to his feet.

"Wait, Papa, listen. Every time George does something wrong and he feels bad, he goes down in the basement."

"I didn't know that." Mr Bean sat down again.

"It's like, Papa, when I feel bad I go in the bedroom and shut the door. When Jenny feels bad, she goes out and skips. When George feels bad, he goes in the basement and sits on the bottom step."

"Why does George feel bad? What has he done?"

"I don't know."

Mr Bean gave her another stern look.

"I really don't know that."

"I think I know," Mrs Bean said in a quiet voice. She stood in the door of the kitchen.

"You know, love?"

"I think so."

"Will you please tell me? Everyone in this family seems to know about the Beans but me."

Mrs Bean took two steps into the living-room.

"While George was drying dishes . . ." Mrs Bean said. She paused.

"Go on, love."

"Well, when George was drying the dishes, he let it slip that I was getting dishes for my birthday."

Anna gasped.

Then there was a silence.

Finally Mr Bean said in a puzzled voice, "George is giving you dishes for your birthday?"

"No, Sam, you are."

"Me?"

Mrs Bean nodded. Anna did too.

"Where did George get the idea that I was giving you dishes?"

Mrs Bean turned to Anna for the answer. Anna said, "Jenny told us."

"Where did Jenny get the idea I was giving your mother dishes?"

"You told her."

"I told her no such thing."

"Jenny showed us the package in the wardrobe."

"There is a package in the wardrobe. I admit that. And it is for your mother. I admit that. But the package does not contain dishes."

"It doesn't?"

"No, I always give your mother a present for herself. I would not give her dishes. Have I ever given you dishes?"

"No."

"And I never will," Mr Bean said with pride.

"But Jenny said—"

"Never mind what Jenny said." Mr Bean turned off the radio in the middle of a song. He started for the door.

"Where are you going, Papa?"

"I am going to the basement to get my children."

"Papa—" Anna began.

Mrs Bean said, "Sam, let them come up by themselves."

"I'm sorry. They are my children and they have been in the basement long enough. I want them home."

He went out into the hall.

Mrs Bean said, "I'm coming, too."

"Then hurry, love."

And they went down the steps together.

Four Beans in the Basement

"After you," Mr Bean said as he opened the basement door for Mrs Bean.

"Thank you."

Mrs Bean stepped around him. Together they peered into the darkness.

"George?" Mrs Bean called softly. Then she said to Mr Bean, "I can't see him, can you?"

Mr Bean found the light switch on the wall. He turned on the light.

George and Jenny were sitting on the bottom step. Jenny turned around. She said, "Hi."

George did not turn around. He stared straight ahead, at the basement.

"Children, it's time to come up now," Mr Bean said.

Jenny looked at George. He shook his head.

"I want to come up," Jenny admitted, "but George isn't ready yet."

"George," Mr Bean said, "You can stop worrying. I am not giving your mother dishes for her birthday."

When George heard that, he turned around. His mouth opened in surprise. "You aren't?"

"No."

"But Jenny said—"

"I know what Jenny said, but I am not giving your mother dishes."

Jenny jumped up.

"But, Papa, you told me it was dishes."

"I did not tell you it was dishes. Think back. What exactly did I say?"

"I don't want to tell you in front of Mama. It's her surprise."

"Go upstairs, please, love."

Mrs Bean said, "I will go upstairs if you all promise you will come too. I don't like it when my husband and children are in the basement."

"I promise for all of us," said Mr Bean.

Mrs Bean said, "Five minutes." Then she went upstairs. Mr Bean turned back to Jenny. "Now, what did I say – exactly."

"Well, I asked you what the box was – it was a big round box – and you said it was Mama's present."

"And then?"

"And then I said the present has to be round

because the box is round," Jenny said, remembering.

"And what did I say?"

"You said, 'That's using your head.'"

"Then what?"

"Then I said, 'I bet it's dishes.' They were the only round things I could think of."

"And what did I say?"

"You winked."

"Then what?"

"Then I said, 'I bet they have flowers on them.' You winked again."

"Jenny, when I wink, that does not mean that you are right. When I wink, it means 'Maybe . . . maybe not.'"

Jenny said, "Oh."

Mr Bean said, "You should know too that I love your mother far too much to give her dishes for her birthday."

"Then it's not dishes? Really?"

"That's right. It is not dishes."

"Oh, I'm so glad, aren't you, George?"

George said, "Yes."

Jenny ran up the steps. Halfway to the top she paused.

"Aren't you happy, George? You didn't ruin the birthday after all."

George said, "Yes."

"So come on."

George got up. He started up the stairs. He paused at the top.

Mr Bean was holding the door open for him. George said, "Papa, will you do me a favour?"

"If I can, George."

"Papa, please don't tell me what the present really is."

"I won't, George."

"Don't even give me a hint."

Mr Bean turned off the light.

"Don't worry, George. I won't."

Mr Bean closed the basement door.

Then Jenny started up the steps with George and Mr Bean behind.

Beans on the Pavement

"Where are you going, George?" Anna asked.

It was Saturday morning – Mrs Bean's birthday.

George glanced at the kitchen. "Just out."

"Where."

"Out!"

"Don't you want to help me make the cake?" Anna asked.

"I've got to go out," George said. He glanced again at the kitchen. "Remember? I've got to get the flowers!"

Anna whipped off her apron. "I know where there are some flowers – Oak Street. I saw them yesterday. I'll show you."

"Just tell me. I'll go by myself."

"I want to go."

"I'm not going to pick them out of somebody's garden, if that's what you're thinking."

"That's not what I'm thinking," Anna said. She pulled on her sweater. "I just feel like walking down Oak Street."

"Don't you have to make the cake?"

"I'll make it when I get back."

Anna and George went down the steps and out of the flat. They walked quickly down the pavement. George was looking for flowers. Anna was looking at the people.

They had walked four blocks when suddenly Anna grabbed George's arm.

"That's him!"

George looked up, startled. "Who?"

"Him!"

George looked down the street. He didn't see anybody but two men in front of the barber shop and a red-headed boy across the street.

"Him!" Anna said. "The boy!"

"What boy?"

"The red-headed boy, the one I was telling you about. Don't you remember? The one that

calls me Anna Banana."

"Oh, that boy."

"Yes, that boy, and there he is!"

"So?"

"He's crossing the street, George. He's seen me. He's coming!"

Anna gripped George's arm tighter.

George said, "Let go of my arm. You're hurting me."

"I know why he's coming over," Anna said. "He's coming over to call me Anna Banana. I know that's what he's going to do. You'll hear him. I can feel myself getting mad."

George pulled at his arm. He said again, "Let go!"

Anna did not hear.

She said, "Pretend we don't see him, all right? Don't even look up!"

George nodded and Anna yanked his arm. "I said not to look."

"I wasn't looking. I was nodding! Anyway, let go of my arm."

"Look down at your feet. Look down!"

George looked at his shoes.

He could hear the red-headed boy's footsteps. The red-headed boy was coming closer and closer.

Anna squeezed his arm tighter and tighter.

Then the red-headed boy's shoes came into George's view. Even if he had not seen the shoes, he would have known the boy was there.

Anna was squeezing his arm so tight he thought it would never work again.

He was afraid to say, "Let go of my arm," because every time he said it, she squeezed tighter. He gasped with pain.

George waited. He was holding his breath. He knew Anna was, too.

Both of them were waiting for one thing: "Anna Ba-naaaaaa-na."

Then, George hoped, he would get his arm back.

Still they waited.

The boy was right beside them.

Now! Now was the perfect moment for him to say, "Anna Ba-naaaaaa-na."

The boy said nothing.

George kept waiting. Anna did too.

The boy passed. His footsteps started getting fainter.

The red-headed boy was leaving.

George strained his ears. Now he could not hear any footsteps at all.

The red-headed boy was gone.

Finally George glanced at Anna. She was still listening.

George said, "He's gone. You can let go of my arm now."

"He couldn't be gone."

"Well, he is."

"He couldn't be. He didn't go, 'Anna Banana'. Maybe he's hiding in a doorway or something."

"Can I look?"

"All right, but don't let him see you."

George raised his head and looked around, He glanced over his shoulder. The red-headed boy was not hiding in a doorway. The red-headed boy was gone.

"Nope, he's gone for good."

Anna lifted her head. "Are you sure?" She, too, checked the doorways.

George said, "I guess you fixed him. He probably didn't like it the other day when you looked at him like he wasn't there. Oh, thanks," he added as she released his arm.

He began to rub it. His hand tingled as it

came back to life. He moved his fingers to see if they still worked. It would be hard to pick flowers if they didn't.

"I guess not," Anna said.

"You can stop worrying now. Mama was right. That boy will never call you Anna Banana again."

"I guess not."

"Oh, look, Anna, there are some flowers on that wasteground. Are those the ones you were talking about?"

"I guess."

"It's all right if I pick them, isn't it?"

"I guess."

"They aren't weeds, are they?" He didn't wait for an answer. He ran and picked the flowers. He had a nice big bunch, and they were yellow. Yellow was one of his mother's favourite colours.

George ran back to Anna. She was standing exactly where he had left her.

"Look! Now I know they're not weeds. They're too beautiful."

"What?"

"The flowers, Anna, Mama's birthday flowers."

"They're very pretty, George. Are you ready to go home now?" she asked in a flat voice.

"If you are."

"Yes, I'm ready to go home."

"This has been my lucky day," George said as they started walking. He looked at Anna. "And it's your lucky day, too."

"What makes you think that?"

"It's my lucky day because I found the flowers. And it's your lucky day because the red-headed boy will never bother you again."

An Arm Full of Beans

The Beans sat around the kitchen table. Each Bean had a piece of birthday cake.

George finished first. He said, "That was very good cake."

Mrs Bean said, "Tell Anna. She was the one who made it."

"Anna, that was very good cake."

Anna said, "Thanks."

"Very, very good cake."

Mrs Bean said, "Anna, I believe George is hinting for another piece."

"Oh, sorry. Pass your plate, George."

George passed his plate, and Anna put a slice of cake on it.

"Anna, I believe George is right. This is the best cake ever," Mrs Bean said. "What do you think, Sam?"

"I've never had a Bean cake that wasn't good."

"Another piece, Sam?"

"A small one." Mr Bean patted his waist. "Then we'll go in the living-room, love, and you can open your presents."

"You already have mine," George said.

George pointed to the flowers in the middle of the table. He wanted to make sure his mother was not expecting anything else.

"I know, George." Mrs Bean reached out and touched her flowers. "And yellow ones. I love yellow flowers."

"Anna, you are quiet tonight," Mr Bean said. "And you aren't eating your cake."

"I'm not very hungry."

"Is anything wrong?"

"No, Papa, nothing's wrong."

George swallowed. "No, nothing's wrong. In fact, everything is the opposite of wrong!"

"What do you mean by that, George?"

"Didn't Anna tell you about seeing the

red-headed boy this morning?"

Jenny said, "No, you didn't say a word." She leaned eagerly across the table. "What happened?"

"Anna, tell them about the red-headed boy,"

George said. "Remember? About us seeing him and about him not calling you Anna Banana? Tell them."

"I don't have to tell them," Anna said. She sighed. "You just told them for me."

"I want to hear it from you," Jenny said.

Anna sighed again.

"I want details," Jenny said. "How you looked at him . . . how he looked at you . . ."

"Well," Anna said, "there's nothing to tell. He walked past us and didn't say anything at all. Not one word."

"Not even Anna Banana?"

"Not even that."

"Still, I wish I'd been there," Jenny said. "How did you look at him, Anna? Did you look at him like I showed you?"

"I didn't look at him at all."

"I knew my idea would work," Jenny said proudly. "Now I know I'm going to be a famous actress."

"Yes, it worked all right," Anna said.

She pushed back her chair.

"Is everybody through?" she asked. "I'll start doing the dishes."

"The dishes can wait," Mrs Bean said. "I'm going to open my presents."

"I know, but I have to go to the library and get a book for history."

"I'll do the dishes myself," Mr Bean said. "Come. Let's watch your mama open presents."

The Beans went into the living-room.

"Open mine first," Jenny begged. "Mine is home-made so you may not like it."

"I love home-made things," Mrs Bean said. "You know that."

"And it's not as long as it should be. I ran out of yarn."

Mrs Bean unwrapped the package. She held up the small knitted square.

"I like it! And I needed one."

"It's a pot holder," Jenny said.

"I know."

"I knitted it myself."

"Did you? And I didn't even know you could knit!"

"Maria taught me."

"Here's mine," said Anna.

Mrs Bean unfolded Anna's card. She said, "A poem! Oh, Anna, you read it."

"If you want me to. It's called 'Mama's Birthday'.

"Everything loves Mama's birthday.
The candles shine extra bright.
The cake is feathery light.
And when we sing,
'Happy birthday, dear Mama',
The words sound just right."

"Why, Anna, it is beautiful. Thank you."

"You're welcome."

Mr Bean picked up the round box with the ribbon on top. "Now, here are your famous dishes, love."

"Papa, you said it wasn't dishes," Jenny said.

"And it isn't. That was a Bean joke." Mr Bean handed the box to Mrs Bean. "For you, love."

Mrs Bean took the box and smiled. "Now I know it's not dishes. It's too light." She gave it a gentle shake. "And it doesn't rattle."

Mrs Bean undid the ribbon. She lifted the top of the box. She folded back the thin white paper.

"Oh, Sam."

Mrs Bean reached into the box.

"Oh, Sam," she said again.

She brought out a soft, grey furry hat.

"Sam, is it real fur?"

"Oh no," he said. "It just looks real."

"Oh, Sam!"

Mrs Bean got up and went to the mirror. She put on the hat.

"Oh, Sam."

"Mama, can't you say anything but, 'Oh, Sam'?" Jenny asked.

Mrs Bean turned around. The hat was on her head. Tears were in her eyes.

"You saw me looking at those furry hats in the shop window, didn't you, Sam?"

"Once or twice," Mr Bean said.

"You knew how much I wanted one."

"I thought you might like to have one."

"Thank you. Oh, thank you."

Mrs Bean ran across the living-room and hugged Mr Bean. Then she waved them all into her arms. Jenny – George – Anna – Mr Bean. Her arms were full of Beans.

"This is the best birthday I have ever had in

my life," she said.

"Mama, you say that every year," Jenny said.

"And every year I mean it," Mrs Bean answered.

Beans at the Library

Mrs Bean was standing in front of the mirror, admiring her hat. George was washing the dishes. Mr Bean was looking through some records. Anna was putting on her sweater.

Jenny was not doing anything. "Anna, can I come to the library with you?"

Anna did not answer.

"Please, Anna, I want to get some books. I don't have anything to read."

"Oh, were you talking to me?"

"Yes. Can I come to the library with you?"

"Sure," Anna said, "but I don't want to stay long."

"I want to get three books, and I know which three books I want."

"Then let's go."

Anna went down the steps as if she didn't want to go to the library at all. When they were on the pavement, Jenny said, "I wish I'd been there this morning."

"This morning?" Anna asked without interest.

"Yes, you know, when you and George saw the red-headed boy."

"Oh, that."

"I would have liked seeing that."

"There wasn't anything to see. He walked by like I wasn't there."

"Now you know how it feels."

"Yes."

"I'm interested in things like that. When I get to be an actress, maybe I will be in a play. And maybe it will be a play about a girl and a red-headed boy and maybe—"

"Can't we talk about something else besides red-headed boys?" Anna asked.

"Oh, all right. I thought you liked to talk about them."

"Well, I don't. So, change the subject."

Jenny thought for a moment. Then she said, "Do you think Mama liked my pot holder or do you think she was just being nice."

"I think she liked it."

"I know she liked your poem and I know she liked George's flowers and she loved Papa's hat. But I'm not sure about the pot holder."

"She loves things that we make."

"Yes, but it was really only half a pot holder. It should have been about that long—" She broke off. "What's wrong?"

Anna had tripped on a crack in the sidewalk. "There he is," she said.

"The red-headed boy? Where? Is that him going into the library?"

"Yes."

"Anna, he doesn't look anything like I thought he would. I thought he would have bright red hair and an ugly face. He's cute."

"Cute! I don't see anything cute about him."

"Anna, if we hurry, we can go in the door at the same time he does."

"What good will that do?"

"Then I'll get to see you look at each other like you aren't there! Please!"

"Well, all right."

Anna and Jenny ran up the library steps and got there at the same time as the red-headed boy.

The red-headed boy turned and looked at Anna.

Jenny's eyes shone. She looked from him to Anna, then back at him. She grinned. She couldn't wait to see them look at each other like they weren't there.

Anna said, "Hi, Robert."

The red-headed boy said, "Hi, Anna."

Anna said, "I didn't know you came to this library."

The red-headed boy said, "I didn't know you did either."

Anna said, "I have to get a book for history."

The red-headed boy said, "So do I."

Anna said, "Want me to show you where the history books are?"

The red-headed boy said, "Yes."

Anna said, "Come on."

And they went into the library.

Jenny's mouth dropped open.

She had never been so disappointed in her life. They had looked at each other. And, worse, they had talked to each other. And he even had a name! Robert! Anna hadn't told Jenny she knew his name. It wasn't fair.

Jenny went back to the shelves and got her three favourite books. She was glad they were all there. At least that wasn't a disappointment.

She checked them out and then she waited for Anna. Anna and the red-headed boy – Robert – took a long time getting their history books. They took a long time checking them out.

Jenny waited because she had a lot of things to say to her sister. She wanted to say, "You didn't tell me you knew his name. That wasn't fair. And you didn't even try to look at him like he wasn't there. And why didn't he at least say, 'Anna Banana'?"

But when Anna started for the door, the

red-headed boy came with her.

"Anna, we have to go home," Jenny remind-
ed her.

"What's the hurry?"

"On Saturday nights Papa sings with the
record player – you know that. I want to hear
him."

The red-headed boy said, "I'll walk with you,
Anna."

Jenny said, "We can walk home by ourselves,
thank you. We always do."

"Jenneee." Anna poked Jenny with her history book.

Jenny said, "Ow."

"If you're in such a hurry, you can go on by yourself," Anna said.

"No, I'll go with you two."

Jenny grinned to herself. Maybe she would be in a play some day, and the play would be about a girl and a red-headed boy walking home from the library together. Maybe she could pick up some tips.

Anna and the red-headed boy went down the library steps. With her three favourite books in her arms, Jenny followed.

Beans at Home

Jenny ran into the living-room. "Guess who we saw?" she asked.

Mrs Bean was sitting on the sofa. Her birth-day hat lay on her lap like a kitten. Mr Bean was putting a record on the record player.

"Tell us quickly," Mrs Bean said. "Your father is getting ready to sing."

"We saw the red-headed boy!"

Mrs Bean said, "Oh dear, I hope he didn't upset Anna. I hope he didn't call her Anna Banana."

"He did not."

"Good."

"He called her, 'Anna', like that. And she called him, 'Robert', like that."

"Oh?"

"Mama, here's the way she looked at him."

Jenny struck a pose.

"And here's the way he looked at her."

She struck another pose.

"And here's the way I looked at both of them."

She let her mouth fall open in disgust.

Mrs Bean smiled and patted the place beside her on the sofa.

"Sit with me."

"All right, but it was so disappointing. It's very unusual for me to be disappointed in a

Bean, but this week two Beans have disappointed me.

"Oh?"

"First, George – for breaking a promise. Then, Anna – for the red-headed boy."

"Where is Anna now?"

"She's on her way up the steps – very, very slowly, pulling herself along with the railing. Want me to show you how she looks."

"No."

"I can do it perfectly."

"I'm sure you can," Mrs Bean said. She touched one finger to her lips. "This is one of my favourite songs."

Jenny sat beside her mother. She wiggled until she was comfortable. "Still," she said, "I'd rather be a disappointed Bean than no Bean at all."

Mrs Bean nodded in agreement.

Mr Bean stood at the record player, quietly waiting for the music to begin.

When it started, he lifted his head and sang. *"Oh, sole mio!"*

Anna came into the living-room then. George did too. And the five Beans enjoyed the song together.

Betsy Byars
Beans on the Roof

I love the roof
And that's the truth

A poem by Jenny Bean (with a little help from Anna and George and Mama and Papa).

There's only one problem when Anna decides it's fun to write poems on the roof of her house . . .

. . . all the other Beans want to do it too!

A selected list of titles available from Macmillan and Pan Books

The prices shown below are correct at the time of going to press. However, Macmillan Publishers reserve the right to show new retail prices on covers which may differ from those previously advertised.

Beans on the Roof	*Betsy Byars*	£3.50
Tales of a Fourth Grade Nothing	*Judy Blume*	£3.50
Superfudge	*Judy Blume*	£3.50
Fudge-a-Mania	*Judy Blume*	£3.50

All Macmillan titles can be ordered at your local bookshop or are available by post from:

Book Service by Post
PO Box 29, Douglas, Isle of Man IM99 1BQ

Credit cards accepted. For details:
Telephone: 01624 675137
Fax: 01624 670923
E-mail: bookshop@enterprise.net

Free postage and packing in the UK.
Overseas customers: add £1 per book (paperback)
and £3 per book (hardback).